(6) Till

The electrifying serial concl...

In *The Slobberers*, Rory and Dawn were chased into the night by horrifying bone-sucking slobberers – only to be confronted by killer sheep and a bus trip from hell in *Battering Rams*.

Kamikaze frogs at home in *Croaked*, a crazy snail, and a boy who was a *Dead Ringer* for Rory meant the quest for the truth had to continue.

But Howard didn't have the answer to the mystery, and Rory's apple-man grew monstrous long tendrils . . . *The Creeper* was trying to kill them.

To solve the mystery and save their family, they must find Karl. What awaits them in the abandoned refinery – a new beginning or a horrible end?

Find out in *Till Death Us Do Part*, the final thrilling instalment of this wicked serial. You'll never forget it.

Wicked!

6 Till Death Us Do Part

Morris Gleitzman and Paul Jennings

PUFFIN BOOKS

PUFFIN BOOKS

Published by the Penguin Group
Penguin Books Ltd, 27 Wrights Lane, London W8 5TZ, England
Penguin Putnam Inc., 375 Hudson Street, New York, New York 10014, USA
Penguin Books Australia Ltd, Ringwood, Victoria, Australia
Penguin Books Canada Ltd, 10 Alcorn Avenue, Toronto, Ontario, Canada M4V 3B2
Penguin Books (NZ) Ltd, 182–190 Wairau Road, Auckland 10, New Zealand

Penguin Books Ltd, Registered Offices: Harmondsworth, Middlesex, England

First published in Australia by Penguin Books Australia 1997
Published in Great Britain in Puffin Books 1998
1 3 5 7 9 10 8 6 4 2

Copyright © Greenleaves Pty Ltd and Creative Input Pty Ltd, 1997
All rights reserved

Set in Cheltenham

Made and printed in England by Clays Ltd, St Ives plc

British Library Cataloguing in Publication Data
A CIP catalogue record for this book is available from the British Library

ISBN 0–140–38995–4

ONE

Gramps stared at my face and screamed. He looked terrified. I staggered backwards on the little underground jetty.

What was going on? I looked around wildly and tried to make sense of it. Water gurgled along the underground drain. Rats scampered in dark corners. We were alone and helpless, but I couldn't see anything to scream about. There was no sign of the terrible apple-man. There was no mouldy-faced horror glaring out of the darkness.

Or was there? Gramps was looking at me as if *I* was the enemy.

'What's the matter, Gramps?'

I gasped. 'I won't hurt you.'

'Get away. Get away, spy,' yelled Gramps. His spindly legs began to shake and for a moment I thought he was going to fall back into the dark water below.

'Gramps, it's me – Rory,' I shouted. 'You're just seeing things again.'

'Rory?' he said. 'Rory? You can't be Rory. You're, you're . . . ugly.'

I held my hands up to my face and touched the skin. My flesh was all loose and wrinkled. It was horrid to touch.

But there was something else. Something terribly wrong. I couldn't feel the pressure of my fingers on my cheeks. I pinched my nose. Nothing. My fingers could feel my face. But my face couldn't feel my fingers.

I frantically touched my chin and lips and explored the curve of my mouth. Everything was still there but nothing seemed the same. My own face felt as if it belonged to someone else.

Invaders.

Cold fear washed over me. I had been invaded. Evil germs were taking hold. It all flashed through my mind. Everything that had happened. The slobberers infecting me back in the wrecker's yard. Me passing the disease on to the sheep. And then my mum catching it from the lamb. The frogs looking for Mum. The snail and the vine that wanted to infect Howard. The apple-man. The horrible germs that were following my blood-line. Trying to kill me and my relatives.

From animal to human being. From human being to animal. And plants. It used them too. Frogs, apple-men, snails, vines. All wanting me and mine.

The germs were changing my appearance. Feeding on my fear of the mouldy apple-man. The fearsome foe who had grown to human size and was trying to kill us. Now the wicked illness had changed me so much that Gramps couldn't even recognise me.

'It *is* me,' I shouted. 'It *is*. It's me – Rory.'

Gramps moved forward carefully. He was still scared of me. He peered at my face. 'Okay,' he said nervously, 'I'll test you out. If you're Rory you'll be able to answer a few questions.' He bent down and picked up a rusty iron bar which lay on the jetty. 'If you get them wrong you cop this, Apple-spy.'

I took a few steps backwards and stood precariously on the edge of our little refuge. One more step and I would fall back into the rushing stream. 'Anything,' I said. 'Anything.' I nodded my head furiously.

Gramps began to quiz me. 'What did I eat that I shouldn't have?'

'A snail,' I yelled.

'Wrong,' shouted Gramps. 'You're not Rory at all.'

He started to walk towards me with the iron bar held above his head. I didn't know what to do. Gramps was old and tottery. I could have knocked him over but I didn't want to hurt him. I didn't want to get clobbered with the iron bar either. He came towards me. He was going to let me have it.

I tried to think. What was the answer? What could it be? 'A compass,' I shouted. 'You ate the compass.'

Gramps lowered the iron bar. But he still wasn't sure that the ugly person facing him was really me.

'What did I throw in the mouth of the frog?' he demanded.

'Salt.'

'Who put the apple-man spy in the car boot?'

'Howard. And . . . me.'

'What is your father's name?'

'Karl.'

'Who is the best Gramps in the world?'

'You are,' I shouted. I threw myself into his arms. He was smiling. He believed me. He knew it was really me. He hugged me tight.

'Rory,' said Gramps. 'You're in a bad way, mate. We have to get help.'

I passed my hand over my rotting face. 'I'm terribly sick,' I said faintly. 'And no one can help me. But I've got one thing to do while I still can. I'm going to find my dad. I have to see his smile just one more time.'

Gramps gave my hand a squeeze. 'This is only a battle,' he said. 'The war's not over yet. We'll find the answer. You wait and see.'

I walked around the small jetty looking for a way out of the drain. We could go back the way we had come but I wasn't sure that we could make it in the strong current. Neither of us was strong enough. Or we could head upstream, further into the tunnel. But where did it go and how far was it?

Then I noticed a steel ladder on the wall across the water. It stretched up above our heads into another huge chimney-like tunnel. The ladder had at least a hundred rungs and it led up to a steel door. It was a long way to the top.

Suddenly a rusty squeal filled the air. The door opened and light filtered into the shadows above. Someone or something was standing in the doorway.

'The apple-spy,' whispered Gramps.

'The mouldy apple-man,' I said hoarsely.

It was him. It was him. Our deadly enemy was looking down at us. He was high above and I couldn't make out the details. But there was one thing for sure. He had something white and hairy and foul where his head should have been. Just the thought of that terrible being made my stomach churn. I felt as if maggots were eating my last store of courage.

But I still had a little bit left. I snatched the iron bar from Gramps' hand and hurled it up at the mouldy apple-man. 'Take that,' I screamed.

The bar hurtled upwards, turning and twisting through the air. Then it clanked harmlessly into the wall halfway up the ladder and began to fall. It fell with a splash into the water below.

The mouldy apple-man quickly ducked back and slammed the door.

Once more we were alone.

I could feel defeat and despair gnawing away inside me. I looked at my hands and arms. The flesh was loose and sagging. The germs were spreading, spreading, spreading. I couldn't bear to think what might be ahead.

Suddenly the despair turned to anger. My mother was infected. And maybe my father. And now that mouldy spectre wanted to spread the disease and kill my brother. And anyone else who got in its way. Even poor old Gramps. How dare it. I didn't care about myself any more. I was filled with rage.

'Okay, Apple-head,' I yelled into the shadows above. 'So you want a fight, do you? Okay, here I come.'

'You can't go up there,' shouted Gramps. 'It's a trap.'

'Just watch me,' I said.

Gramps tried to hold me back but I pulled away. I lowered myself into the water and waded into the stream. I felt my foot touch something hard. The iron bar. I bent down and picked it up. Then I splashed my way across to the steel ladder on the other side.

'Don't, Rory boy, don't,' pleaded Gramps.

I ignored him and started to climb. One, two, three, four rungs. Suddenly my fingers touched something hanging on a rung above my head. I stopped and tried to work out what it was.

'What's up?' yelled Gramps.

'I've found something,' I said. Then I began to scream. And scream and scream.

'Hands,' I shrieked. 'There's a pair of hands hanging on to the rungs.'

'Don't touch them,' yelled Gramps. 'I'm coming.'

Touch them? I couldn't touch them, not in a million years. They weren't just hands. They were sucked-out hands. With no bones or muscles. Flat, empty skins. Some poor person had had their innards sucked out. Only the dried-out hands were left, still gripping the ladder. Suddenly I realised what the furry slippers were that I had seen at the entrance to the drain. Sucked-out rat skins.

Something terrible was in the water below. 'Hurry,'

7

I yelled at Gramps. 'Hurry.'

Gramps struggled slowly across the stream and pulled himself up onto the ladder. He stared at the hands which gripped the rung like a pair of frozen ...

'Gloves,' said Gramps.

'What?' I yelled. 'They look like hands to me.'

'Can't be,' said Gramps.

'Why not?' I shouted.

'They've got no fingernails.'

I suddenly felt stupid. Thinking that gloves were hands. A wave of relief washed over me. But it didn't last for long.

'What about the rat skins?' I yelled. 'What about those? There are slobberers here, Gramps.' I threw the gloves into the stream below and continued to climb. Gramps followed, grasping each rung weakly with his knobbly fingers.

Up, up, up. I stared down. The dimly lit jetty looked like a child's toy in the water way below. On I went until at last I reached the door at the top. There was no handle. I knew that on the other side – somewhere – was the mouldy apple-man.

I tried to stop a terrible thought entering my mind. A thought that had been trying to surface ever since my appearance started to change. I didn't want it out in the open. I didn't want to know what this disease was going to do to me.

I had to stop myself thinking about it. Action was better than thoughts. Anything but face the truth. I clung on to the top rung with one shaking hand and desperately beat on the door with the iron bar.

'Come on, mouldy Mister Apple-head,' I yelled crazily. 'Come on, slobberers. Come and see what I've got for you.'

TWO

I lay as still as a corpse on the hospital trolley. The sheets draped over it hid me from view, but I was still taking a huge risk.

I gripped Mum's shoe. It had saved me from killer sheep and evil strangling apple-man roots. Would it save me from two nurses and a doctor?

They were wheeling me along a corridor in the huge city hospital. 'Heard the news?' I heard the doctor say. 'This morning's triplets. Two of them were two kilos but the third was only one kilo and a bit.'

The nurses made sympathetic noises. 'Is the littlie okay?' one of them asked. 'Fine,' said the doctor. 'Mum and dad are over the moon.'

I gritted my teeth and forced myself to stay hidden on the base of the trolley. I wanted to leap out and give the doctor and nurses a good shake. I wanted to tell them that Eileen and Howard's ward was where their attention was desperately needed, not the maternity ward.

'Families aren't only loving parents and two-point-five children,' I wanted to yell at them. 'Families are also step-families struggling with jealousy and sadness and evil diseases.'

But I didn't because my family was one of those and the only way I could save them was to get out of the hospital without being caught.

I spent the rest of the trip down the corridor planning the details of how I'd save them. I knew I didn't have much time. The infection was killing Eileen and that meant it was doing the same to Rory, with Howard not far behind. They might only have a few hours.

I made a list in my head of everything I had to do in that time.

1. Find Rory's dad.
2. Get him to say where the infected slobberers came from.
3. Tell the doctors so they could find out more about the infection and discover a cure for it.
4. Wait for the results.

It seemed a lot. And what if we couldn't find Rory's dad? I prayed Rory and Gramps had found some clues at the refinery. But then what if Rory's dad didn't know where the slobberers had come from? I didn't want to think about that.

I didn't get a chance to.

The trolley stopped suddenly. I heard the doctor and nurses walk away. I decided to risk lifting a sheet to see where I was. Before I could, the trolley swung round and a male voice started humming.

There was a bump and a jolt and I heard lift doors closing. We were going down. I had a horrible thought. What if we were going to the hospital laundry? What if they just chucked their sheets in the washing machine on hot without checking for stray bedsocks or children?

The lift jolted and we clattered out. Then the trolley stopped.

Silence.

It wasn't the laundry. I couldn't smell steam or detergent or stain remover or fabric softener.

The humming started again. It was getting fainter. The man must be moving away from the trolley. Should I run for it now?

I decided to wait, just to be safe. Time was tight but another couple of minutes wouldn't make any difference. It wasn't as if Rory and Gramps were facing immediate danger.

That's when it hit me.

I should have thought of it before. In the quarantine ward. When I realised Howard was infected.

Howard's apple-man. If the root infected Howard, it probably infected his apple-man too. I remembered the crunch when Howard hurled his apple-man at the tendril clamped round his ankle. Okay, he and Rory dropped the apple-man down a mine shaft, but so what? Infected worms could turn into slobberers. Infected sheep could turn into steel killers. An infected apple-man could easily turn into something horrible and climb out of a hole and come after us.

The figure I'd seen at the refinery. The evil figure running along the fence. I hadn't imagined its mouldy wrinkled apple-skin after all.

I had to warn Rory and Gramps.

Now.

I flung the sheet aside and scrambled off the trolley. Bright lights. Trolleys everywhere. In the far wall, an open roller-door. A cloud of insects and a black square of night.

'Hey.'

A man in a white smock. Turning from a bench. Holding a spanner.

'Please,' I begged, backing away, banging into trolleys. 'My step-brother and my Gramps. They're in terrible danger.'

DAWN

The man ran at me, then his eyes widened and he stopped. He was staring at me, horrified. What was wrong? Did he know Gramps? Perhaps they'd been in the war together.

Then I realised. He was staring at my skin. At the purple and yellow blotches I'd drawn on to get into the quarantine ward.

'It's okay,' I shouted as I sprinted for the door. 'It's only texta.'

I dashed through a car park full of ambulances, up a ramp and into the street. It was a street I hadn't seen before. I didn't care. There was a bus in it, waiting at traffic lights. I hammered on the door. The driver let me in. He must have sensed I was related to someone in the bus-driving business.

'I'm never going back,' I said to him as I dug in my pocket for money. 'That face-painting class was a joke.'

He looked at me for a long time. Then he hit the accelerator and we jolted into the night.

The other passengers were all staring at me. I considered asking if any of them was an ex-commando with a couple of hours to spare, but decided against it.

We were hurtling down dark streets and I realised I didn't have a clue where we were going. I also realised I didn't have any money for my fare.

I turned to the driver again. 'I shouldn't have been going to face-painting classes anyway,' I said. 'Not with the homework I've got. I'm doing a huge project on why the oil refinery closed down. You know, that one over there.'

I pointed through his window.

'You mean over there,' he said, pointing in the opposite direction.

Luckily someone wanted to get off at the next stop. I dashed down the steps after them. 'Hey,' yelled the driver. 'That's seventy cents.'

I felt bad, jumping off without paying, specially as he'd pointed me in the right direction. I made a mental note to post seventy cents to the bus company if I was still alive next pocket-money day.

I ran until my lungs were on fire and I kept on running.

In the distance I heard a siren. Were the ambulances out looking for me? I told myself not to be dopey, then ran across a park to throw them off the scent.

I shouldn't have done that. The park had twisty paths and by the time I came out the other side I'd lost my direction. I kept running. Every dark street looked the same. I sprinted round a corner, praying the refinery road would appear.

It didn't.

DAWN

I gasped air and sobbed desperate tears. The same desperate tears as Rory was probably sobbing as the evil mould-dripping apple-man lurched towards him.

I pressed Mum's shoe to my forehead. 'Help me, Mum,' I whispered. 'I need you. Even if you were the bad person people say you were, I still need you.'

That's when I heard it. The hum of fast traffic in the distance. The freeway.

I reached it in a few minutes. There was a pedestrian bridge. As I staggered to the top, my mind was racing. Gramps had turned left off the freeway to get us to the refinery. We'd been heading towards the city centre.

I scanned the horizon and saw the city skyscrapers lit up against the night sky. I turned to my left and peered into the darkness. And just made out, faint and distant, a familiar forest of dark shapes silhouetted against the electric haze.

The refinery.

It took me another half-hour to find the refinery road. The pub where I'd asked directions was closing up. I slipped past it in the shadows and stumbled along the road, beyond where the streetlights stopped, through the darkness to the towering, rusty, chained refinery gates.

Gramps' car was parked where we'd left it. I threw

myself on the back seat and sobbed tears of exhaustion and relief and fear.

Then I pulled myself together. I let Gramps' handbrake off and pushed the car slowly and painfully over to the gates. I climbed on to Gramps' roof trying not to scratch his duco and flung the tarpaulin and blankets from the boot over the barbed wire at the top of the fence.

No sound came from the hulking darkness of the refinery. No rattle and clatter as Rory opened old filing cabinets looking for his dad's forwarding address. No swearing as Gramps banged his head on cranes. No evil rasping breaths as the apple-man crept up on them.

I wouldn't have made it over the gate without the thought of Rory and Gramps to keep me going. Finally I dropped into the mud on the other side.

I crouched and listened. Nothing.

I gripped Mum's shoe in one hand and Gramps' tyre lever in the other and wondered if I should call out to warn Rory and Gramps. I decided not to. No point in letting the apple-man know they were there.

As I picked my way between the huge storage tanks, I peered desperately into the darkness. I didn't want to miss seeing Rory and Gramps. If the apple-man had already found them, they might be somewhere nearby.

Unconscious.

Or dead.

I felt panic in my throat and tried to force those horrible thoughts out of my mind.

They were replaced by another horrible thought.

What if I came face to mouldy face with the appleman?

I could run. I could try to save myself. But I knew I wouldn't do that. There was no point. I'd never get back over the fence.

Plus there was another reason.

I'd had enough. I'd already lost my mother. I wasn't losing anyone else. Not without a fight.

I peered through the tangle of pipes and ladders ahead of me. Suddenly I almost wanted to see that ugly, white, mould-covered face gleaming in the moonlight.

'You evil slimebag,' I whispered. 'If you've killed my step-brother and my Gramps, you're dead meat.'

I stuffed Mum's shoe inside my shirt, gripped Gramps' tyre lever and stepped into the darkness.

THREE

I clung desperately to the top of the ladder and beat on the door until I was exhausted. But it was no use. There was no way of opening it from my side. I looked down and groaned.

Gramps was still climbing slowly up the ladder. 'Hang on, Rory boy,' he called in a faint voice. 'I'm coming.'

'Go back,' I screamed. 'I can't get in.'

Gramps didn't take any notice. He just kept coming.

I kept banging the door with the iron bar but it was shut tight. The filthy stinking apple-man was on the other side. I just knew he was. I was filled with rage. 'Apple-head,' I screamed. 'I'm going to rip your ears off.'

Without warning the door above me swung inwards and a dim glow of light filtered into the air above us. A shadowy figure stood there. 'Got yooooooo . . . ' it screamed in a savage voice. It stepped out.

19

Onto nothing. The sound choked off as the figure began to fall. A hand grabbed my jeans and almost tore me away from the ladder.

'Let go,' I shouted. 'Let go, you scumbag.'

My fingers began to slip. The weight was terrible. In any second we would fall down onto Gramps and the three of us would plummet to certain death. I started to kick at the head beneath me.

The figure below screamed in fury. 'Where's my step-brother, you overgrown apple?'

'Dawn?' I gasped. It was her. It really was. My step-sister. Big bad Dawn. I was so happy. Help had arrived.

Dawn grabbed the ladder with one hand and managed to get a foothold. Then she started to pull at my feet, trying to dislodge me from the ladder. She was trying to kill me. She didn't recognise me.

'Stop it,' I screamed. 'It's me. Rory.'

Dawn stared up through the shadows at my twisted ugly face.

'Bulldust,' was all she said.

'It *is* him, sweetheart,' came a weak voice from below.

Dawn looked down and stared in amazement.

'Gramps?'

'The one and only,' he chuckled.

Yes – chuckled. I couldn't believe it. With all this

danger. With all this trouble. The three of us stuck up a ladder in deadly peril. In the middle of all this he could still chuckle. Good old Gramps.

'Rory,' shouted Dawn. 'Where's the apple-man? I heard someone scream. I thought he was killing you. I rushed here to save – ' She was interrupted by a loud squealing noise.

'Quick,' I said. 'Go down.'

But I was too late. With a tortured howl of grinding metal the top of the ladder came away from the wall. Bolts and chunks of concrete fell into the darkness then splashed into the water below.

'Aaghhh,' we all screamed together.

The ladder bent backwards and yawed away from the wall. We were stranded in mid-air as if we were at the top of a flagpole. A flagpole that at any moment was going to topple.

'Don't move,' yelled Gramps. 'Don't move, whatever you do. The rest of the bolts will give way.'

We couldn't go up. And we couldn't go down. And there was no way we could hang on for much longer.

Suddenly I saw something – a long piece of thin timber was making its way towards us out of the door. Was it trying to push us over? Or was it the hand of help? I couldn't see who was holding the other end. Could it be Dawn's dad Jack come to save us? Maybe it was the police or a caretaker.

Was it a friend?

Or was it the evil, stinking mouldy apple-man?

I grabbed the end of the waving strip of timber with one hand and hung on. Slowly the ladder began to move back towards the door. Someone – something, was pulling us in. We were nearly there. Closer, closer.

Yes, yes. A cold damp hand reached out for me. I grabbed it and was heaved into a room. I lay gasping on my stomach and heard Dawn and Gramps scramble to safety. I sensed that it was Apple-head that had reeled us in. But I didn't want to look at him. Like a little kid who thinks that they can't be seen when they have their eyes closed, I refused to look.

But I had to. I rolled over and stared. My heart missed a beat. The blood froze in my veins. We all gasped and shrank back in fear at the horrible sight.

The wicked eyes of the appalling apple-man stared at us through a coating of wet, horrible mould. He held out his long crooked fingers and began to stagger towards us.

I was paralysed. I couldn't move. Couldn't think. Like a timid mouse before a snake I just lay there and quivered in terror.

Dawn sprang to her feet. She bent down and picked up a length of chain and threw it at his rotting face.

'Take that, you putrefied pile of poop,' she screamed.

The chain tore a track through the white mould on its head and revealed folds of sagging flesh. In an instant the mould spread across the track and reclaimed the skin for itself.

The rotting figure staggered forward. It ignored Gramps who was feebly trying to regain his breath. It ignored Dawn as she searched desperately for something else to throw. It was me that it wanted. The iron bar fell from my trembling fingers as the mouldy creature staggered forward with outstretched hands. I fell back helplessly and pushed myself away. Trying to force myself into the wall – through the wall – to safety.

Suddenly it leapt and pinned me to the floor. It reached into the blue refinery uniform and tore something from a hidden pocket. It waved it in my face.

I blinked and tried to see what the monster was holding. It was, it was. It couldn't be. Howard's little apple-man. The horrible creature was clutching Howard's apple-man. Even in my terror I could see that.

The little apple-man's head was split open. And was covered with worm tracks.

This rancid, mouldy figure that was pinning me down was not Howard's apple-man grown huge and come to life.

RORY

So who was it? What was it?

'Rory,' it croaked. 'Oh, Rory.'

I looked into that decaying face – and for the second time in one week saw myself in another's eyes.

I let out one terrible, wonderful word. One wailing, despairing question.

'Dad?'

FOUR

Even when Rory said the word, I couldn't believe it. Rory's father was the apple-man? This horrible pathetic stomach-turning walking fungus was Rory's dad? I didn't want to believe it.

Yes, I was in shock. Yes, I was dazed and trembling. But I still had a mind of my own.

I wouldn't believe it.

Then I saw the tears. Running down that awful face. Making little rivers through the white mould. And I knew they were a dad's tears.

Rory knew it too. He threw himself into Karl's arms. 'Dad,' he sobbed. They held each other for a long time. It was a dad's hug all right. I blinked back my own tears.

Poor Rory. He'd waited so long to see his dad again. He must have imagined this moment a million times. But not even after eating pickled onions at midnight could he

25

have dreamed it would be like this.

I wished I could do something to make it better for them both. 'I'm sorry, Mr Singer,' I said. 'I'm sorry I called you a putrefied pile of poop.'

Gramps struggled to speak. He was in shock too. 'She – she's sorry she chucked the chain at you too,' he stammered. 'Childish high spirits, you know.'

Karl didn't even hear us. He was staring at Rory. At Rory's own sagging face which now had its own patches of mould.

'Oh, son,' croaked Karl. 'I tried to keep you away. To scare you off. But all the time it was too late.'

He put his face in his hands and puffs of white powder floated off him as his shoulders shook with grief.

'It's okay, Dad,' sobbed Rory. 'You didn't know my apple-man was infected when you sent it.' He paused, then added in a tiny voice. 'Did you?'

Karl took a painful breath. He shook his head and held up the remains of the apple-man. 'I only discovered it was infected tonight,' he said. 'When I took it from your car.'

'Point of order,' said Gramps. 'It's actually Howard's.'

Karl stared at Gramps with narrow bloodshot eyes. Gramps shifted uncomfortably. 'Sorry,' he said, 'Shouldn't have interrupted. Sorry.'

Karl swayed and for a second I thought he was going

to faint. Rory grabbed him. Karl gave an anguished moan. 'Not my other son too,' he croaked. 'Don't tell me Howard's infected too.'

I didn't want to tell him. Karl looked so sick and weak I was worried he wouldn't survive any more bad news. But a father had a right to know. So did a brother and a step-Gramps.

'I'm afraid so,' I said quietly. 'I've just come from the hospital.'

Rory and Gramps both groaned. Karl put his face in his hands again.

'He's not very far gone,' I said. 'Nowhere near as bad as . . .' I stopped.

Rory put his arm round his father's shoulders. 'Mum's infected too,' he said softly. They held each other for a long time. My eyes filled with tears.

After a bit I pulled myself together. We needed information. Something was nagging at me. 'Mr Singer,' I said, 'how did you know the apple-man in the car was infected?'

'I didn't at first,' said Karl. 'I went to your car to scare you away. I looked in the boot for some brake fluid to burn a message in the duco.'

Karl paused for breath. Gramps gestured for him to continue. 'It's okay,' said Gramps. 'It's an old car.'

'I found the apple-man in the boot,' continued Karl.

'I saw the worm holes in it. And when I got back, there were creatures here.'

I stiffened. Creatures?

'Slobberers,' said Rory.

My insides froze. Suddenly I was aware of every tiny noise as I strained to hear something I'd hoped I'd never hear again.

The slurping, sliming sound of slobberers.

I looked at Rory and he looked away. I wanted to yell at him. He and Howard hadn't ditched the apple-man after all. They'd hidden it in the car. And now the slobberers were back.

I made myself control my anger. Blame wasn't going to save our family. Anyway, I sort of understood. There was no way I'd have ditched Mum's shoe under any circumstances. I gave Rory's hand an understanding squeeze and turned to Karl.

'Mr Singer,' I said urgently. 'We need to know everything you can tell us about the infection.'

'I'll explain everything,' said Karl, 'but not here. It's too dangerous with the creatures about.'

He didn't need to persuade us. We helped him along a dripping metal tunnel that stank of diesel fumes. As I gripped his arm to take his weight I was shocked by how cold and saggy his skin was.

I didn't let him see me flinch. I wouldn't if it had been

my dad, and Karl was Rory's dad which was almost the same.

As we made our way down the tunnel, moving through faint patches of electric light and pools of darkness, Rory told him about our run-ins with the first slobberers and the steel sheep and the frogs and the snail and the root. Karl didn't say much, just groaned sometimes. He might have said some other stuff, but I wasn't paying that much attention.

I was listening for other sounds. Sucking, slobbering sounds.

The tunnel suddenly ended. In front of us was a metal wall with a round door in it. The door was studded with rivets and had what looked like a steering wheel in its middle.

Karl tried to turn the wheel. Rory and Gramps helped him. 'Air lock,' wheezed Karl. 'I chose it because nothing can get out. Luckily for us nothing can get in either.'

The door swung open. We stepped through.

We were in a room shaped like the inside of a giant baked-bean can. Loose planks of wood made a sort of floor. Standing on it were a few bits of office furniture.

Gramps swung the door shut and turned a wheel on the inside.

'Dad,' said Rory, close to tears. 'You can't live

in here. It's too unhealthy.'

'No, son,' said Karl quietly. 'You've got it wrong. I'm too unhealthy to live anywhere except in here.'

Rory started to protest, but Karl held up a big spongy hand. 'I'll explain,' he said.

He sat down slowly on a narrow bed made from two filing cabinets and a padded insulation jacket like the one on our school water heater. He tried to continue but his head dropped and he slumped against the wall.

'He's unconscious,' said Gramps. 'Medics on the double.'

We laid him gently on his bed. Rory and I squeezed his hands. It was like squeezing cold cooked cauliflower.

'Don't die, Dad,' begged Rory.

'Rations,' said Gramps.

The only food I could find was in tins. I opened a can of sliced peaches and moistened where I thought Karl's lips would be with the juice.

After a few seconds Karl opened his eyes.

'Sorry,' he said weakly. 'I must have blacked out. I've been doing that a bit lately.'

'Mr Singer,' I said gently, 'we need to know how the infection started.'

Karl sighed and I could see he was making his mind

go back to a place it didn't really want to go. I hoped the infection would help his memory like it had Rory's and not damage it like Eileen's.

'About six years ago,' Karl began slowly, 'we were stripping the refinery before it closed down. I was the safety officer. It was my job to make sure nobody got hurt or infected. Pretty funny, eh?'

I hoped he wouldn't try to laugh. He didn't. He just took a wheezy breath and carried on.

'I had to inspect an old tanker before a demolition team went in to pull out the pumps and stuff. That's where I found it. In one of the bulkheads. White mould.'

He stopped to catch his breath.

Rory gave him a sip of peach juice.

'I'd never seen anything like it,' continued Karl. 'Did some tests. Didn't seem to be toxic, so I cleaned it out and didn't think any more about it.'

'Mr Singer,' I said quietly, 'were any of the other workers infected?'

Karl shook his head. 'None. I checked later. Dunno why they weren't. I was probably the only one who touched the mould.'

My brain was racing. Something clicked. 'Were you very angry in those days?' I asked.

Karl looked at me for a long time. 'Yes,' he wheezed finally. 'I reckoned it was my wife's fault our marriage had ended. Eileen blamed me for having Howard adopted, even though we'd both made the decision. I was very angry with her.'

I looked at Rory. He was upset at what he was hearing, but he knew why I'd asked the question.

'When the refinery closed five years ago,' continued Karl, 'I went back to be near Rory. I didn't know I was infected. When I started to get sick, I tried to get treatment. The doctors told me it was a virus but they didn't know how to cure it. I knew it was the mould. Bits would sometimes grow between my toes. I tried to cure myself with health food. Organic vegies. Goat's milk. One day my goat Ginger ate one of my thongs and went crazy. Chewed her way into the drawer where I kept some of Rory and Howard's old baby clothes. Ripped them to shreds and didn't touch anything else. Then she ran off after the school bus.'

I stared at Karl. My head was spinning as I digested this.

Karl looked up at Rory. 'I realised then that the virus was after you and Howard,' he said. 'I had to leave, for your sakes. I came back here to the refinery to try and find a cure. I couldn't tell you in case you followed. That's why I sent you both the apple-men. So you wouldn't forget me. Stupid. It was stupid . . .'

Tears made new irrigation channels through the

mould on Karl's cheeks. He struggled for each rasping breath.

Rory gripped his hand. 'It wasn't stupid, Dad,' he sobbed. 'It wasn't.'

They were both so sad I wanted to stop the questions and hug them. But I had to press on. I could see Karl wouldn't be able to talk for much longer.

'Mr Singer,' I said urgently. 'You've been infected for five years. Rory's been infected for only three days. Yet he's almost as sick as you. Can you think of anything that has slowed down your infection?'

For what seemed like an hour Karl just struggled for breath. Then at last he spoke.

'Blue mould,' he whispered.

We all leant forward.

'Blue mould?' I said.

'In the tanker,' he croaked. 'In the sick bay. I've been growing it. Only small amounts, though. Kills the white mould.'

Gramps and I looked at each other excitedly.

'Then the white mould kills it,' continued Karl.

Gramp's face fell.

'Doesn't matter,' I said. 'It's better than nothing. I'll go and find it.'

'Me too,' said Rory.

'No,' gasped Karl. 'Too dangerous. Creatures.'

DAWN

I pretended I hadn't heard that. To myself as well.

'Before we go,' I said to Karl, 'one last question.' I couldn't go without asking it. 'The goat and the bus,' I said. 'When my mother died. Tell me what happened, please.'

I held my breath. Karl sat up. Then he muttered something and slumped against Gramps.

'He's unconscious again,' said Gramps. He listened to Karl's chest. 'I don't think he's going to come out of this one for a while. I'd better stay with him, I was in the tank corps. You infantrymen get the mould at the double.'

'But what did he say?' I yelled as Rory and I headed for the door.

'He said "Watch out for the queen",' said Gramps. He gave Rory a sympathetic look. 'I'm sorry, Rory, but I think he might be going a bit senile.'

FIVE

I left Dad's room with an aching heart. I was in the grip of hopeless grief and despair.

Dad was dying. I kept remembering the old Dad. The one with the kind, handsome face. The one with white teeth and smooth skin. Now he was a germ-riddled wreck, hardly alive. Unconscious. Helpless, and covered in a greedy invading mould.

And me. What about me? I was getting weaker all the time. My face and skin were sagging and collapsing more with every passing minute. The virus was eating away at me. I couldn't see myself but I knew that I must be incredibly ugly. Normally a person's face just looked unhappy if they were angry or sulky or whatever. But those feelings were like fertiliser to the virus. All the bad thoughts I had ever had. All the wicked things I had ever done were like food for the germs. My hateful

thoughts were written on my face.

But maybe there was hope. Just a tiny hope. Maybe we could find the blue mould. And maybe it could save me and the others.

Maybe.

Dawn kept her distance. And I knew why. She could hardly bring herself to look at me, let alone touch me.

We made our way down a steep ramp and found ourselves in the middle of a group of oil storage tanks. Tiny-looking ladders spiralled around each one leading up to giddying heights above.

'Which way to the dry dock?' asked Dawn.

'Why?' I asked.

'Your dad said the mould is in the hulk of a ship. An old tanker. It will have to be in dry dock.'

'How would I know?' I snapped. I'm just an ugly, infected step-brother. You're only coming with me for one reason.'

'Not that again,' said Dawn.

She made me so angry. 'You want to be there at the death knock. Just in case I hallucinate. Just in case I see what happened to your mother. You even had to go and worry my dying father with it. You are so selfish.'

'I do want to know, Rory,' said Dawn. 'But I want something else too.'

'What?' I said scornfully.

'I want to help you. I want to find the blue mould. If there is such a thing. I want you to go back to normal.'

'Don't you like the way I look?' I spat out. 'Don't you want to come close to your worst nightmare?'

'It doesn't matter what you look like,' said Dawn. 'Even if you have got a face like a dag on a sheep's bum, it doesn't mean that you're not still the same person.'

'Thanks,' I said sarcastically. 'That makes me feel a lot better.'

We stared into the dark night. A cold drizzle soaked through our clothes.

Twisted ladders and huge chimneys filled the spaces between the oil tanks. At their feet tangles of pipes fought for space. The whole refinery was like a dead rusting monument to wickedness.

In the distance I heard a bird squawk. 'A seagull,' said Dawn. 'The dry dock must be that way.'

We trudged forward through the darkness. Two lonely figures. Frightened, small and hopeless.

'What did your dad mean by the – '

'Queen?' I broke in. 'Probably just some other bossy female.'

Dawn said nothing. We threaded our way through the dead refinery peering into every shadow. Hoping,

hoping, hoping that slobberers were not waiting for two juicy kids.

'There it is,' said Dawn. We both stared at the deserted oil tanker. Huge and rusting in the dry dock. Propped up by hundreds of wooden beams, it stood alone, abandoned like Noah's ark after the Flood. We perched there on the edge of the dock at deck level and looked down at the silent propeller and the useless rudder.

'How will we ever find a bit of mould in a monster like that?' I said in a defeated voice.

'Listen,' said Dawn quietly. 'What's that?'

We looked up to where the noise was coming from. 'Rats,' I whispered.

Hundreds of rats were running up a rope on to a crane high above our heads. They were squeaking and squealing in terror. They wanted to get off the ship. A terrible smell filled the air. My knees shook as I watched the wretched rodents. 'I can't take much more,' I choked. 'I just can't.'

Dawn tried to cheer me up with a joke. 'Rats always desert a stinking ship,' she said.

I peered down into the dry dock beneath the hull and saw something else. It looked like thousands of pairs of old slippers had been thrown out of one of the port-holes. I knew straight away what they were.

'More rat skins,' I gasped. 'Sucked-out rat skins.

There are slobberers around here somewhere.'

We both stared up at the rickety gangplank that led on to the ship and shivered. Neither of us wanted to go.

'Come on,' said Dawn. 'Don't think about it.'

I couldn't figure out if she was incredibly brave or just stupid. 'Think of the rats,' I said. 'How would you like to end up like that? Sucked out.'

'Think of your mum,' said Dawn. 'Think of your father dying of a terrible disease. Think of Howard. Think of . . .'

'Okay, okay, okay,' I said. I hung my head in shame. We had to find the blue mould. If there was any such thing. Otherwise everyone I loved was going to die. I pushed past her and headed up the gangplank. At the top was a roughly painted sign saying:

**KEEP OFF!
DANGER
CONTAMINATED AREA**

I laughed wildly.

'Rory,' said Dawn. 'You're hysterical. Pull yourself together.'

'I'm already contaminated,' I said. '*I'm* the danger.'
I cackled away like a crazy chook.

The ship seemed dead. All the useful parts had been
stripped away and it was only a hulk. There would
have been no way that we could have gone into the
black insides of that ship. Except for one thing.

A long electrical lead with dim lights glowing from it
led down a steep ladder.

I had a hunch. 'Dad did that,' I said.

Dawn didn't ask me how I knew. She was listening to
something. 'I thought I heard a slurp,' she said. 'Maybe
we should get help.' I couldn't see her knees but I knew
that they must have been knocking. Like mine.

Suddenly she started climbing down the ladder.
'Come on,' she said.

I hobbled towards the ladder and followed her. I felt
as if my body was a heavy load. I was dragging my
infected flesh around. Taking it where it didn't want to
go. It was almost as if the germs inside my body were
trying to control me. And stop me going.

At the bottom of the ladder was a corridor. A bat-
tered sign pointed to the dining room in one direction.
The lights led the other way. Dawn took a curious step
into the darkness. 'Aagh,' she screamed. 'What's that?'

'Yuck,' I said. 'That's the worst stink in the world.'
I was so scared. Something awful. Something evil was

down that passage. Dawn swallowed her own fear and tried to cheer me up. She was gutsy. Trying to pretend that she wasn't scared.

'Reminds me of Lester Green's halitosis,' she said. 'Only a million times worse.'

'Huh?' I said.

'Bad breath,' explained Dawn. 'There wasn't a girl in the school who would kiss him.'

I was just going to say something rude when we both froze on the spot.

'Hhhhcccchhhssshh.' A horrible deep breath. Like a monster snake about to strike. And then a worse sound. One I had heard somewhere before. A terrible, gobbling, sucking noise came from the direction of the dining room.

We both fled in the other direction, following the lights without any idea of where they might take us. We scrambled down stairs and around corners. I lost track of how far we ran following those lights. But there was one thing I did know. We had not passed one other door or passage. We had only two ways to go. Back. Or forwards. We could go back and try to sneak past the dreadful slobbering noise. Or forwards into the silent unknown depths of the hulk.

'What *was* that thing?' I yelled when we finally stopped.

'From the smell,' said Dawn, 'and the hissing and sucking, it could be – '

'Look,' I shouted.

It was the sick bay. The door had a round handle on it like a safe. And just above that was a small glass window with a light above it. We had found what we had come for. Dad's experimental laboratory. Maybe we could find something that would save Dad and Mum and Howard and . . . me. The answer to all our prayers.

We hoped.

I stood on tiptoes and stared into the window. Then I screamed. The most ugly, rotten, decayed face in the world was looking back at me. A face with hateful watering eyes. With sagging skin and patches of white mould and twisted dirty hair. With rotting teeth and bleeding gums.

The face screamed back. It was scared of me.

It *was* me.

I was looking at my own reflection in the glass.

I sagged down like a sack of jelly. Even if we found the blue mould, my life wasn't worth living. I could never leave that ship. I could never face another person. I had the ugliest face in the universe. The virus was ripping into me. Turning me into a monster.

I was too ashamed to look at Dawn. No wonder she was keeping her distance. I sank down on to the metal floor and pulled my windcheater over my head. I wanted to crawl into a hole and never see another person as long as I lived. I wanted to stick my head into a dunny and flush it away.

How could Dawn even bear to look at me?

At that very moment an awful wet spattering sound filled the air. It reminded me of the time the year seven boys had a competition to see who could spit the furthest. Only this was worse. 'Spit, spit, suck, spit.' Wet and bubbling. Horrible. Horrible. Somewhere back along the corridor.

SIX

I **tried to ignore the** distant slobberer sounds as I gripped Mum's shoe and pulled the sick-bay door open. An avalanche of washing powder knocked me over.

I floundered around on my knees in the torrent of white granules. I tried to crawl away, but they poured out with such force I ended up sprawled on my stomach.

'Rory,' I screamed. 'Help.'

Finally the torrent stopped. The stuff was everywhere. In my hair. In my mouth. I was half buried in it.

'Good one, Worm Boy,' I spluttered. 'This isn't the

sick bay, it's the ship's laundry supply store.'

Rory didn't reply. Once I'd got the washing powder out of my eyes, I looked over to where I'd last seen him.

He was huddled on the passageway floor, his windcheater

pulled over his head. Laughing at me, probably. I felt like going over and giving him a good shake. Instead I made myself remember that he was sick. And that the virus must have infected the part of his brain that knew about good manners.

Something was weird. I smacked my lips. The washing powder didn't taste like washing powder. It didn't smell like washing powder either.

That's because, I realised with a sudden jolt of panic, it wasn't washing powder.

It was white mould.

'Aagh,' I screamed. I staggered to my feet and shook my hair and frantically brushed myself down.

A shower. I needed a shower. A big ship like this must have heaps of showers. Then I remembered what Karl had said. The ship had been stripped for demolition. What good was a shower without taps and water?

Anyway, it was hopeless. Even if I scrubbed every grain off myself, it had still been in my mouth.

The horrible truth sank in. This wasn't Karl mould that fed only on him. Or Rory mould that fed only on Rory. This was the original mould that had started the whole nightmare.

And now the virus was inside me. The virus that had infected Karl, that had created the slobberers, was inside me. Now the cycle would start again. I'd infect something and it would infect Gramps. And he'd infect something and it would go after Dad.

And soon our whole family would be dead.

I sank to my knees. Oh, Mum, I thought. Perhaps you were the lucky one, dying first. At least you didn't have to see faces you loved going mouldy in front of your eyes.

I glanced over at Rory. He was still huddled against the wall with his head in his windcheater. I was glad. I didn't want him to see me blubbing.

I wanted Mum. I wanted to be on her bus kneeling with my head in her lap so she could stroke my hair between gear changes. I wanted to be there when she drove off the cliff into the river so I could see why.

Why she'd died.

Then a thought hit me. The virus that was inside me was the same virus that had given Rory his hallucinations. That had helped him remember what happened on the bus up until just before Mum died.

Now I was infected, perhaps I'd have an hallucination. Perhaps at last I'd be able to find out why.

Heart thumping, I screwed up my eyes. 'Come on,' I said to the virus. 'Show me.'

Then another thought hit me. The only reason the virus had been able to bring back Rory's memories of the bus was that he'd been on the bus in the first place. He'd seen Mum's death.

I hadn't. The virus couldn't give me memories of something I hadn't seen.

I grabbed a handful of mould and flung it angrily away. 'Stinking, scumbag virus,' I screamed.

There must have been quite a draught on that half-demolished ship because the tiny grains of mould seemed to float in the air. In the faint gleam of Karl's makeshift lighting system they seemed to glow. And some of them glowed blue.

I grabbed another handful of granules and studied them. No wonder I'd thought it was washing powder. In amongst the white grains were blue ones.

'Blue mould,' I yelled. 'Rory, I've found the blue mould.'

If the blue mould had slowed Karl's sickness from three days to five years, perhaps it could also cure it. Perhaps it could save us all.

Frantically I started trying to collect it. Only about one in every hundred grains was blue. I lifted one up between my fingertips. Before my horrified eyes it turned white.

I picked up another one. It turned white too. Was I doing that, by touching it? Rubber gloves. I needed rubber gloves. Even sailors must have done washing-up.

Then I saw the horrible truth. The blue grains were dying without me touching them. They were appearing from nowhere, bursting into life, then almost immediately turning white. The white mould was killing them.

'Stop it,' I screamed at the white mould. 'Stop it.'

Desperately I tried to pick out several blue grains so I could put them together and they could draw strength from each other away from the white predators.

My fingers wouldn't move fast enough. Big, clumsy fingers. I wanted to chop them off. Why did I have big clumsy fingers when Mum's had been so slim?

I smashed my fists down into the white powder, causing a mini-avalanche. When the grains had stopped tumbling, something familiar was left poking out.

Mum's shoe.

I stared at it. The colour looked different. Instead of scuffed, watermarked brown, it looked almost blue.

I saw why. All the grains sitting on it were blue. And they were staying blue.

Excitedly I picked a blue grain out of the white heap and tried to add it to the ones on the shoe. Before I could let go of it, it had turned white. I tried to flick a blue grain on to the shoe with my fingernail. No good.

I tried to scoop blue grains up with the shoe. Hopeless.

My neck ached with frustration. I felt like giving up and going back to punching the white mould. But something Dad always said popped into my head. 'If at first you don't succeed, stop and think.'

Then I remembered what Karl had said. About trying to grow blue mould. That must be where the blue grains were coming from. His experiments in the sick bay.

I waded through the mould into the sick bay. The small room was waist-deep in white powder. There were bunks on one side and shelves on the other. The shelves were piled high with jars and soft-drink bottles. All full of white mould. Karl's failed experiments.

I swore at the jars and bottles. Until I realised what I was doing. My anger was turning the blue grains on Mum's shoe white. I shook them off and took deep breaths and remembered what Dad said about not giving up till you'd searched the back paddock.

I examined the shelves again. And there, high on the top shelf, I found them. Three small Vegemite jars. One containing a dried-up piece of cheese. One half-full of water. One stuffed with leaves and twigs. And each one with a lump of blue mould in it about the size of a Smartie.

Hands shaking with excitement, I carefully lifted the

jars down. Would this be enough to cure us all? Even as I asked myself the question, I knew it wouldn't. It probably wasn't even enough to cure one infected person, or Karl would have used it on himself.

I knew what I had to do. It was a risk, but my family was dying and I didn't have time to be cautious. I unscrewed each jar and tipped each tiny lump of blue mould into Mum's shoe.

Then I waited.

In less than a minute the blue lumps started to grow. 'Yes,' I screamed. 'Yes.'

The lumps were already the size of Maltesers and still growing. 'Good on you, Mum,' I yelled happily.

I stopped yelling. Something strange was happening. The blue mould was creeping over the entire surface of the shoe, inside and out. The shoe was completely blue.

And getting lighter. Not in colour, in weight.

The blue mould was eating Mum's shoe.

'No,' I screamed. 'No.'

Cupping the crumbling shoe in both hands, I waded frantically out of the sick bay.

'Rory,' I yelled, staggering over to him. 'Stop fooling around. I need your help.' With my foot I dragged the windcheater off his head. And gasped.

His face was terrible. I'd almost got used to what the

virus had done to it before, but this was worse. Much worse.

Even worse than Karl.

Rory's tiny breaths sounded like milkshake fighting its way up a very thin straw. His eyes were closed.

I crouched close to him and as I did I saw that in my hands was just a pile of blue powder. Mum's shoe was gone. I felt grief surging up, but I locked it down with my throat.

'Rory,' I said, 'don't die. I've got some blue mould. Don't die.'

His eyes fell open. They flicked wildly around.

'The goat,' he shouted.

I didn't bother looking behind me. I knew there was no goat on the ship. And I knew Rory wasn't dying, not yet.

He was on the bus.

SEVEN

The bus was facing the river.

The goat was pawing with its front hooves and stamping. Ready to charge down the aisle.

Mrs Enright had selected first gear and had the clutch pressed to the floor.

My father was banging desperately on the door trying to get into the bus.

And I was screaming. 'Dad, Dad, Dad. It's really you.'

He was yelling something and trying furiously to open the door. What was he saying? Something about a boat? No it wasn't that.

'Watch out for the goat,' he shouted. 'Don't touch the goat.'

I threw a quick glance down the bus. The goat was charging. Its eyes glowed horribly. Its face was almost human. As if it knew who we were. It thundered down the aisle with its horns lowered. What was it up to? Was it attacking Mrs Enright?

Crack. I felt the bone break under my jeans. My leg twisted sideways at the knee. The pain was terrible. I screamed in agony and fell to the floor. The goat half jumped, half fell over me and skidded on into the back of Mrs Enright's seat and jolted it forwards so that her legs were crushed up under the steering wheel. It had enormous strength.

'Get out, Rory,' Mrs Enright screamed. 'Get out. I can't reach the gear lever. I can't hold the clutch. Get out. Now.'

The goat backed up over me and positioned itself for another charge. Its horns were aimed right at me.

'I can't move,' I screamed. 'I can't move. My leg is broken.'

With a sudden crash Dad burst into the bus.

'Get him out,' screamed Mrs Enright. 'Get Rory out. I can't hold the clutch much longer. We're going into the river.'

Dad threw a horrified glance at the goat which was thundering back down the aisle towards us. Then he snatched a look at Mrs Enright trapped under the steering wheel trying desperately to keep the pedal pressed in. Finally he turned to me. I groaned in agony. My leg was killing me.

Dad didn't know what to do. I could see it in his face.

RORY

He had to decide. Help Mrs Enright get the bus out of gear. Stop the goat. Or pull me to safety. Dad groaned in agony. And made his choice.

EIGHT

Rory opened his eyes. I knew immediately that he was back with me in the passageway of the abandoned ship. Back in his poor twisted infected body.

The bus trip was over.

I knew because his eyes were full of tears.

He didn't speak. He just lay there panting with shallow rasping breaths. He didn't need to speak. I could see the horrible truth in his brimming eyes.

So it was true. All the things people had whispered about Mum. All the things I'd kept locked away in my nightmares. She had been mad. Or drunk. Or criminally careless. She'd hit a goat and tried to turn the bus around on an impossibly narrow road and had killed herself doing it.

Perhaps it was just as well that her shoe was gone. Now I didn't have anything to make me think about her.

I stayed kneeling next to

Rory for a long time, rigid with misery. I knew I should have been trying to make him better with the blue mould, but suddenly it all seemed hopeless.

Tears ran down my face and dripped onto Rory's hand. They seemed to stir him into action. Wheezing, he dragged himself up onto his elbows.

'I know what happened to your mum,' he said.

'No,' I said. 'Please, I don't want to hear the details.'

He told me anyway.

He described how the goat charged into his leg and broke it and rammed Mum's seat so she was trapped behind the wheel.

'Bull,' I said. 'Goats don't bend steel seat supports. Not unless they're . . .' I trailed off, remembering how strong the infected sheep had been. Then I remembered that the goat had eaten Karl's mouldy thong.

'Don't talk,' croaked Rory. 'Just listen.'

I listened. Rory described Mum struggling to keep her foot on the clutch. He described his dad bursting on to the bus and having to decide who to save. He described it all so vividly I could see it as clearly as if I'd been there.

'Get him out,' screamed Mum. 'Get Rory out. I can't hold the clutch much longer. We're going into the river.'

Karl looked at Mum's foot slipping off the clutch.

He looked at the charging goat. He looked at Rory writhing in agony on the floor.

He grabbed his son and dragged him off the bus.

Even before Karl and Rory sprawled into the bushes at the side of the road, the back wheels of the bus were spinning in the mud. The clutch spring had been too strong for Mum's poor crushed legs.

The bus seemed to hang there on the edge of the cliff for a moment. The back wheels flung sludge at the sky. The engine roared. Then the bus shot forward and over the edge.

That would have been enough for me. Knowing Mum had died a hero would have been enough for me. I could have lived happily with that for whatever short time my infected body had left.

But there was more.

As the bus went over the edge of the cliff, the fuel line must have been ripped out by a rock. Suddenly the engine went dead and the bus fell towards the dark swirling river in silence.

Except for one sound. Mum's voice, strong and clear.

'Dawn,' she shouted with the passion and energy that Dad reckoned had made the bedroom windows rattle when I was born. 'I love you.'

Even after the bus had disappeared into the depths of the river, and Karl had dived in after it, Mum's words still echoed inside my head and I knew that from then on I'd have to be dead to stop hearing them.

I slumped back against the wall of the ship's passageway and a storm broke inside me that would have been a match for any storm that ship had ever seen, even in the Atlantic. Tears that had been waiting five years came out in huge shuddering sobs. Tears of sadness. Tears of grief. Tears of love.

They took a long time to pour out, but when they stopped I felt more peaceful than I could ever remember feeling, including being with Dad at Dubbo zoo.

Until I heard a faint, high-pitched rasping.

Rory. He was barely breathing. He stared up at me with dull eyes. The colour and life were draining out of his poor suffering face.

I'd forgotten about the blue mould. While Rory had been telling me about Mum, my fists had been clenched tight. I opened my hands and in each palm was a sweaty lump of blue mould the size of an egg.

I broke a piece off one of the lumps. Then I panicked. How should I give it to Rory. Externally? Internally?

I rubbed the blue mould carefully on to his face. He looked at me gratefully, but the light continued to fade in his eyes.

'Thanks,' he whispered, 'but it's too late.'

I broke another piece off and gently pushed it

through his lips into his mouth.

His eyes closed. His breathing slowed. The blue powder on his face was gradually turning white.

My eyes filled with tears again. 'Oh, Rory,' I said.

He was dying. He'd helped me get my mum back and now he was dying. And there was nothing I could do.

Except what his mum would have done.

I leant forward and kissed him gently on his swollen lips. They didn't feel swollen to me and I didn't feel like his mum.

I felt like a girl who loved him.

Out of the corner of my eye I saw his cheek turning blue. I'd always imagined that when I finally kissed a boy both our cheeks would probably turn red, but his were definitely turning blue.

I peered at them. The blue mould on his face was growing. It was eating the while mould.

Rory's eyes opened. 'Don't stop,' he murmured. I'd always imagined that when a boy said 'don't stop' I'd stop immediately, but on this occasion I didn't. I put a piece of blue mould into my mouth and lay down next to Rory and put my arms round him.

I only gave myself a tiny piece. With Mum's shoe gone we couldn't grow any more. The two lumps were all we had for Karl and Eileen and Howard.

Rory and I lay like that for a long time. As the

minutes passed, and Rory's breathing slowly got stronger, I thought how lucky I was to have a brother like him.

My thoughts seemed to help. His face became less twisted and the terrible marks of the infection started to fade. So I kept on thinking those thoughts and having those feelings.

It wasn't hard. It was much easier than thinking about the slobbering horror that was waiting for us at the other end of the passageway.

NINE

Dawn had kissed me. My first one. Probably hers too. With a kiss she had saved my life.

What had gone on in her mind? Kissing my revolting sagging face. It was a kiss that gave, not a kiss that took. There was nothing in it for her. It was an act of compassion. She was telling me, 'Rory, I care about you. Rory, I don't want you to die. Rory, even though you are infected, I really care.'

She was saying, 'Rory, you are not ugly. Not inside.'

I kept touching my lips and remembering the softness of Dawn's. How could she have done it? How could she have kissed my foul flesh?

I remembered the look of love in her eyes. Not love like in soppy love stories. Not girl-friend love. But the sort of love that you have for a brother. He might annoy you. He might get on your nerves. But you don't want him to die.

And then I realised that was how I felt about her. She was daggy. Sometimes she was bossy. But she was kind. And gutsy.

I didn't love her like a girlfriend. I loved her like a sister.

And she had saved my life. She had put the blue mould in my mouth and it had started to work. I could feel it making me better. But it wasn't enough. The virus had been too strong for it.

Until Dawn gave me the kiss of life. And gave the blue mould what it needed to grow and do its work.

I wanted to ask if her feelings were the same as mine. But I was embarrassed.

'That kiss,' I stammered. 'Did . . .'

'Yes?' said Dawn.

'Did I have halitosis?'

'Rory,' she said. 'This is no time for discussing personal hygiene. We have to get that mould back to your dad. And Howard. And your mum. Before they die of the virus.'

She held up the two precious balls of blue mould – one in each hand. All that was left. But enough. Just enough to save them all. If we could get it back in time.

I suddenly felt terribly guilty. I was so pleased to be getting better and so shocked by the kiss that I had forgotten all about the others.

Dad and Eileen and Howard. They were all dying and I could only think about myself.

We had to take the mould to them. Quickly. Dawn and I were the only ones who could save them. Only the blue mould could kill the virus. And what about poor old Gramps? All alone with Dad. Trying to keep him alive.

'Let's go,' I said.

We started back along the small corridor, following the dim, yellow lights. Suddenly they went out. We were in total darkness.

'Hang on to my belt,' I said.

'Why?' said Dawn.

'So we don't get separated.'

'You hang on to me,' she said.

Boy, she could be annoying. Why did she always have to lead the way? Still, she had saved my life. And kissed me. At that moment I would have forgiven her anything. I grabbed her belt and followed her along the empty, black corridor.

Suddenly she stopped.

'What is it?' I whispered.

'Something's blocking the way,' she whispered back. 'The whole corridor is blocked with flat furry things. A whole wall of them. Someone, something is trying to stop us.'

I put my hand out and quickly pulled it back again. 'Yuck,' I screamed. 'Rat skins.'

'Slobberers have been here,' said Dawn. 'That's what the spitting noise was.'

I tried to pull one of the rat skins out but it wouldn't budge. The skins felt as if they had been cemented together by a sort of sticky wet dribble. It was as strong as glue.

'We'll have to go back to the sick bay and keep going that way,' I said.

Dawn started to make her way back down the corridor the way we had just come. 'I think I know where this leads,' she said. 'And I'm not sure I want to go there.'

But she kept moving on. Sometimes she stumbled. Once she fell. But she climbed back up without a word and went on. And I followed, hanging tightly on to her belt. Suddenly she stopped. And started to sniff.

'It's that smell again,' I said in a shaky voice.

'It's like I thought,' she said. 'This corridor has been going in a circle. It's leading back to the dining room from the other direction.'

'Halitosis,' I said. 'Stinking slobberer breath. Let's find another way.'

'There is no other way,' said Dawn.

I held on to her more tightly and we moved forward

with trembling legs and racing hearts. The smell grew worse and worse. Oh, foul. Oh, disgusting. We were walking to our doom. Walking into the slobberers' nest. I was sure of it. But we had to go on. We had to get the mould to Dad and Howard and Mum.

Now we could hear them. Sucking, sucking, sucking. A revolting sound. The slobberers' wet song of death.

Our legs took us forward. How I don't know. We were like condemned prisoners walking to our doom. Slowly, I began to see details of the passageway. Dim light was filtering through dirty portholes. I could make out the shape of Dawn's head. Morning had arrived.

Up ahead I could just read a sign hanging above a steel doorway. It read:

'What's for breakfast?' said Dawn.

I didn't laugh. 'Listen,' I said. The sucking was much louder.

I shuddered and remembered the sucked-out skin of the dog at the wrecker's yard. But I didn't say anything.

We crept up to the door and peered around the edge.

Nothing could have prepared us for the sight. No one

in the history of the world had ever seen such a sight.

A huge slobberer the size of a whale almost filled the room. It lay on its side revealing four bloated, blue teats. On each teat a baby slobberer sucked greedily.

Babies. Surely they couldn't be babies. Each one was as big as a cow.

'The queen,' I gasped. 'She's feeding them up.'

I knew where that queen had come from. Howard's infected apple-man. And now the queen was gigantic. She must have eaten thousands of rats.

The queen's long wet tongue flicked around the room like the tail of a crocodile. Suddenly she flipped it upwards into the shadowy mass of pipes and pulled down a fat rat. In a second it was gone. Swallowed. Sucked out.

Phoot. She spat the skin out like a bullet and it thunked into the wall.

We crept back down the corridor. 'There's no hope,' I said. 'We'll never get past her. That tongue would suck us up in a second.'

I hung my head. It was useless. There was no other way out. Dad would die. And Mum. And Howard. And in the end Dawn and me. We were trapped like rats in the abandoned hulk.

'Listen, Rory,' said Dawn. 'We have to work together

on this.' Dawn held up her fists and shook the two balls of blue mould at me.

'This would kill the queen,' she said. 'It killed the white mould. It would do the same to the queen.'

I shook my head. 'We'd never get near it,' I said. 'Not with that tongue lashing around. And anyway, if we use the mould up on the queen there will be none left for Mum and Dad and Howard.'

'We could use half of it,' said Dawn. 'We could use one ball on the queen. And keep the other for your family.'

I remembered the frog general. Gramps had killed it by throwing salt into its cake-hole. If we could throw some mould into the queen's gob she might die too.

The thought of that slimy mouth made me shudder. Someone could die throwing the mould into it. And that someone should be me. I took one ball of mould from Dawn and held it in my hand. If the queen ate me she would eat the mould as well. And that would be the end of her.

It was strange really. The virus had nearly killed me. And now I would soon be back to normal. Looking forward to a great life with Mum and Dad. I had defeated death and now I had to face it again. There really wasn't any choice. Dawn had risked her life for me. She'd kissed me, even though she might have become infected. She'd pressed her soft lips against my rotting ones.

Now it was my turn. There was only one thing to do.

'Take off your bra,' I shouted suddenly.

'What?' she yelped.

'Take off your bra.'

'Rory,' she said in an outraged voice. 'Get real.'

She stared at me. Then her eyes grew round. She was remembering. Remembering a silly trick played by a silly boy a long time ago. Without another sound she pulled her arms inside her T-shirt and started to wriggle and jiggle like a butterfly trying to get out of a cocoon.

'Got it,' she yelled. She shot out one arm and held her bra in the air above her head. We both looked at each other, embarrassed. After all, she was my sister. My face felt as red as hers looked.

'Tie it across the doorway,' I said.

We snuck back to the door and I pushed one end over a rusty bolt near the door frame. Then I passed the other end across to Dawn. *Please don't let the queen see it. Please don't let the queen grab my outstretched arm.*

Dawn wedged her end into a broken hinge. The sucking of the babies grew louder but there was not a sound from the queen.

I put my precious ball of mould into one of the cups

of the bra. Just like I had done so long ago with tennis balls.

Suddenly I leapt into the doorway and pulled my slingshot back. 'Take that,' I screamed. I released the bra and the ball of mould hurtled into the air.

The queen saw it. Her eyes darted from side to side. She opened her huge mouth. Then, like an expert batsman, she flipped the ball of mould into the air with her tongue.

It broke into pieces and fell like powder slowly downwards.

My heart fell with it. The queen had beaten us. Hit us for a six.

There was only one ball of mould left. We could try to use it to save ourselves. Have another shot. But then we'd have none left to try and save Mum and Dad and Howard.

We watched in despair as the blue powder floated down.

All over the baby slobberers.

They immediately began to squirm and jiggle. They didn't like it. It was attacking them. Sending them crazy. But they didn't let go of those teats. Not for a second. They began to suck at an enormous rate. Faster and faster. Sucking, sucking, sucking. As if they were dying of thirst. In agony they sucked. Faster and faster. The blue mould was sending them into a feeding frenzy.

The queen let out a furious howl of pain. She shook her fat body like a dying walrus but to no effect. The babies bit harder and sucked even more furiously. They grew and grew as the gorging continued.

And the queen began to shrink. Squealing and thrashing around she tried to rid herself of her terrible offspring.

Dawn gasped in horror. 'They're sucking her out,' she yelled. 'They're swallowing her innards. Drinking her guts.'

I could only nod in amazement. The babies grew larger with every swallow. Now they were the size of cars. They wallowed and wriggled and sucked, in last desperate struggles for life.

The queen gave an enormous hiss and then collapsed like a huge rug onto the floor. They had totally sucked her out. She was nothing but a giant slimy mat.

The monstrous babies continued to suck on the empty teats. But there was nothing left. The meal was over.

Boom. The first baby exploded in an ear-splitting shower of foul, yellow muck. *Boom, boom, boom*. The others followed. They splattered all over the floor and walls.

A silence fell over the dining room. Dawn and I just stood there staring at the scene with mouths hanging open.

I bent down and examined the remains of the babies. 'Looks like curried egg,' I said.

We both started to laugh.

Then we ran over the empty skin and carried our ball of mould along the corridor and up the ladder into the open air.

I was filled with happiness. The mould was curing me. And we had enough for poor Mum. And Dad. And my brother Howard. Everything was great. My real family was going to be together again.

'Dad,' I screamed. 'Mum. Howard. I'm coming.'

TEN

I thought **Rev Arnott** was going to faint when Dad asked him for another wedding.

'But,' he stammered, 'the last one was only five weeks ago.'

'Yeah,' said Dad, 'but it was a bit disrupted so we thought we'd do it again. Plus there's a few people who couldn't make it last time. A step-son I didn't know I had. And my wife's ex-husband.' Dad gave me a grin and ruffled my hair. 'And my daughter wants to be there for the whole thing this time.'

I poked my tongue out at Dad and ruffled his hair.

Rev Arnott mopped his face with a piece of blotting

paper from his desk. He did look very stressed. I realised what it probably was.

'It's okay,' I said. 'None of the wedding party or guests will be contagious. The doctors have given us the all-clear. And I promise there'll be no worms in church this time.'

Rev Arnott looked a bit relieved. I gave him a smile, glad to have helped.

I didn't mention my concern about the wedding.

Last night we had a pre-wedding family dinner. It was a bit of a squash round the table because Gramps invited Ivy Bothwell and we invited Alex and Bob. They're the government men who've been looking after us and keeping the media away. They reckon if word about the virus leaks out there could be a national health panic. I've tried to explain to them how that probably won't happen now the virus has been eradicated, but they reckon people get very tense about health issues.

I know what they mean. A couple of days ago I asked Eileen if she was going back to her bottom exercises and she got extremely tense. I had to give her a very long hug and clean her new bike to calm her down.

Mostly she and I get on pretty well, specially when we do things together like visiting Mum's grave or laying the table for dinner like we did last night.

While we were waiting for Karl and Howard to arrive from their new place across town, Gramps was telling Ivy Bothwell about Mum.

'A hero,' he was saying. 'Gave her life to save a passenger. Pity not more bus drivers are like that.'

I grinned. Gramps had already said that to most of

the people in town, including two bus drivers. He'd even persuaded the local paper to do an article about Mum. And persuaded Alex and Bob to allow them to print it as long as he didn't say anything about the goat being infected.

'Of course,' said Gramps to Ivy Bothwell, 'she got her guts and determination from me. Did I tell you about the time Rory and I wrestled a giant toad?'

'Frog, Wilf,' said Ivy Bothwell. 'It was a frog.'

Ivy told me the other day how she's really attracted to men with failing memories because they don't waste time talking about old cricket scores.

Gramps told the story about the frog again, and Alex and Bob started looking a bit anxious in case Ivy was a reporter for a pensioner's magazine. I was feeling a bit anxious too. Not about Ivy, about Rory.

He was sitting in the corner not saying anything. He's been moody and quiet for several weeks, ever since we got back from hospital. I've asked him what's wrong but he hasn't wanted to talk. Even though the doctors have guaranteed there's no virus left in his body, and his skin is as clear as Karl and Eileen and Howard's, seeing him sitting there so depressed I was worried something was wrong.

Then Karl and Howard arrived and suddenly I was a lot more worried.

Their faces were covered in white patches. My insides froze. Everyone in the room stared in horror. 'Oh no,' whispered Eileen. 'Karl, your face.'

Karl looked at us for a moment, then burst out laughing. 'Relax,' he said. 'It's just paint.'

We gawked at him.

'We've been painting the ceiling of my room,' grinned Howard. 'We ran out of turps.'

Everyone breathed out and started talking all at once.

'Jeez,' said Eileen. 'Don't do that to us.'

'There's turps under the sink,' said Dad. 'Don't get it in my lamb stew.'

'I used to wear a fair bit of camouflage in the war,' said Gramps.

'I've got some news,' said Karl when he'd cleaned himself up. Most of us quietened down when we heard this. Gramps carried on whispering to Ivy Bothwell about boot polish.

'I had a call this afternoon,' continued Karl, 'from the defence department team who are analysing the tanker at the refinery.' Now he had Gramps' attention too. 'They reckon the virus came from an area of the Persian Gulf affected by an underwater volcanic eruption. The tanker took water in there as ballast on its last voyage out to the oilfields.'

'That's just a theory,' said Bob hastily.

'It hasn't been verified,' added Alex, looking nervously at Ivy Bothwell.

We all started talking about underwater volcanic eruptions and how we'd stay well away from them in future. Except Rory. He just sat there looking sadly at Karl and Eileen.

I went and sat next to him.

'What's wrong?' I asked quietly. 'Do you want to talk? We can go out the back.'

Rory shook his head.

'Rory,' I said, exasperated. 'We've fought slobberers and killer roots together. We've saved each other's lives. We've shared a bra. Talk to me.'

His eyes filled with tears. 'It's private,' he muttered. 'Family business.' He got up and went to his room and locked the door.

This morning, when we were ready to leave for the church, Rory wasn't around.

'It's okay,' said Eileen, 'he's over at Karl's.'

But when Karl and Howard arrived here at the church, Rory wasn't with them. I wanted to go and look for him, but the adults made me stay here and Karl went.

The wedding should have started ten minutes ago. Mrs Conti is playing 'Here Comes the Bride' for the fifth time. Mr Kinloch from the Wool Growers' Association is making an origami sheep out of his hymn list.

Rory still isn't here.

Neither is Karl.

It's what I've feared.

ELEVEN

Here I am back on the bus just sitting and looking down the aisle. Nothing much has changed. The seats are still sagging and the broken windows are covered in dust like before. The same tree is growing up through the bonnet outside.

The skeleton of the goat is gone, though. Dad had come and buried it with the dog skin. Just to be on the safe side.

There's lots to be happy about.

Everyone is well again. I am healthier than I have ever been. Even my limp is improving. And Dawn and I are getting on terrifically. She still bugs me some-

times, especially when she comes into my room without knocking. But at school we always stick up for each other. Like the time Dawn put Rick Philpot in his place for repeating that false rumour about my dad being in trouble with the police. She fixed him up real good.

And Gramps. Well, he still keeps thinking he is back in the war and gets things muddled up. But he laughs a lot. He hangs around with Ivy Bothwell. And he and I go fishing together on Sundays and always have a great time. Dawn gets a bit cut about it but she's never said anything.

And Dad. That's the best of all – knowing that he loves me. And on top of that there is something else. It is still a secret but some government research scientists want to buy the blue mould from him. It turned out to be a new sort of penicillin. Howard says that Dad is going to be rich one day. We're both going to get new trail bikes. Fantastic.

So why aren't I happy?

Because I've got a problem, that's why. I've been sitting here churning it over for ages. A few minutes ago I had just started to go over it again when a noise interrupted my thoughts. Someone was coming. A figure stepped up into the bus. I couldn't see who it was because the sun was glaring through the windscreen.

'Rory,' said a voice. 'Dawn told me you'd be here. Why aren't you at the wedding? Everyone's waiting.'

It was Dad. He came and sat next to me. Worried.

I stared at the floor. 'I'm not going to the wedding,' I said. 'I don't want Mum and Jack to get married again.'

'Why, mate? Why?' said Dad. He couldn't believe what he was hearing.

'I want them to get divorced.'

'What?'

'I want *you* and Mum to get married again,' I yelled. 'I want it to be like it was in the old days. When we all had tickle fights. And cooked sausages and eggs together on Saturdays. And went to the market. And you and Mum held hands and – '

'Rory,' said Dad. 'It was all over long ago with me and your mum. We can't get back together.'

'Why not?' I shouted. I could feel tears starting to form in my eyes.

'We don't love each other,' said Dad. 'Not in that way. Not any more.'

'So now I have to choose,' I yelled. 'I have to decide whether to live with you and Howard, or with Mum and Jack. I want you and Mum together. Just the four of us.'

Dad stared out of the window. 'Rory,' he said. 'We've already been through that. You can live with your mum and come and see me any time you want. All you have to do is hop on the bus. Or you can live one week with her and one with me. Or whatever you like. It's up to you.'

'It's not the same,' I said. 'It's just not the same.'

Dad didn't say anything for quite a bit. 'I know it's not the same,' he said. 'But it can still be good.' He looked at his watch. Then he rubbed his hand through my hair. The way he always used to. 'I have to go,' he said. 'We're holding up the wedding. Are you sure you won't come?'

I shook my head stubbornly. Dad stood up and headed off. 'I understand,' he said. 'I'm not going to force you.'

I looked out of the window and watched him walk past the clapped-out Land Rover and out of the broken gates of the wrecker's yard.

He is gone.

After everything that has happened I'm back in the bus where it all started. I want to go to the wedding. I want to join in with the others. I really do.

But I just don't think I can face it.

TWELVE

I thought Dad and Eileen's first wedding was tense but this one has turned out to be even tenser.

Fifteen minutes after the ceremony was meant to start, Rory and Karl still hadn't arrived.

My insides were in a double knot.

Rev Arnott was chewing his lip. Dad and Eileen were staring at the aisle carpet, pale and anxious. The guests were turning round in their pews, whispering to each other. Even Gramps looked worried.

I slid up next to Howard. 'Rory wouldn't talk to me,' I said. 'Did he tell you what's bugging him?'

'No,' said Howard, 'but I can guess. It's not easy,

having more than two parents.'

I nodded.

'It's great having extra ones,' he continued, 'even if they're not all still around, but it can be mighty confusing.'

I nodded again. I could see Howard was thinking about the

couple who had adopted him and then been killed. I wanted to give him a hug, but there are some painful feelings you have to have on your own.

Like the ones I imagined poor Rory was having.

Howard swallowed and blinked. Then he grinned bravely.

'Anyhow,' he said, 'let's look on the bright side. They'll probably turn up for the reception. Rory wouldn't miss party pies.'

I tried to grin bravely too, but I'm not as good at it as Howard.

'Talking of the reception,' said Howard, 'I hope you're going to be gentle with Gavin and Kyle Kinloch.'

I looked at him. Then I turned round and glared at the Kinloch brothers. They saw me and both blushed.

Relax, I said to myself. You've handled slobberers and killer mould. You can handle a couple of year-seven dopes giving you a hard time because you're wearing a dress.

I knew I could. But I still wished my new T-shirt hadn't disappeared. The one I'd been planning to wear with jeans.

I gave the Kinlochs another glare and they went bright red.

Howard leant over to me. 'They're going to ask you for a dance,' he whispered.

I stared at him, speechless.

Then Rev Arnott cleared his throat and explained that the ceremony had to start because he had another one booked in for twelve-thirty.

Dad and Eileen stood up the front with their shoulders slumped and I knew exactly how they felt. How could we be a proper family if we couldn't even do the wedding right?

Rev Arnott started the service, but his heart wasn't in it. Neither was mine. I could see Dad and Eileen's weren't. The only people who looked keen for it to happen were the Kinloch boys.

Rev Arnott said the bit about how if anyone had a reason why these two people should not be joined together in holy matrimony, speak now or forever hold your peace.

The door at the back of the church swung open with a creak.

We all turned. Standing there were Rory and Karl.

I stopped breathing. The church was silent except for the faint tinkling of Gramps' medals. I looked at Rory. Rory opened his mouth. Then closed it again.

'Sorry we're late,' said Karl.

'Don't worry,' said Rory. 'We haven't got a reason why Jack and Mum shouldn't be joined together.'

The whole congregation breathed a sigh of relief.

Dad spoke. 'I have,' he said.

We stared at him, gobsmacked.

Rev Arnott went pale.

'Me and Eileen should not be joined in matrimony,' said Dad, 'before we've thanked our kids for everything they've done to keep this family together.' He looked at me. 'Even when a certain dopey dad didn't take his daughter seriously.'

Everyone in the church breathed another big sigh of relief. Dad and Eileen came over and hugged me and Rory and Howard.

Then Karl did the same.

And Gramps.

When Ivy Bothwell flung her arms round Howard, Rev Arnott suggested that further thanks be saved until after the wedding.

As Dad and Eileen renewed their vows, and said the stuff about being a family till death us do part, Rory and Howard and I looked at each other and we knew that went for us too.

Dad and Eileen gazed at each other lovingly, and something in their faces reminded me of Mum.

This was the moment I'd been dreading. The moment that could ruin everything.

I turned and looked at Karl. The man who'd brought the virus into our lives. Into Mum's life. If I was going to blame anyone for Mum's death, it would be Karl.

I've been looking at him for a long time. He hasn't seen me because he's too busy gazing at Rory and Howard with love, and Eileen and Dad with genuine pleasure.

I don't blame him. He's just a parent doing his best. Like Eileen. Like Dad. Like Mum.

I don't know why thinking that is making my eyes fill with tears, but it is and they're tears of happiness.

Everything's going to be all right.

Well, most of the time.

I've just noticed something about Rory I hadn't noticed before.

He's wearing my new T-shirt.

The End

Other books by Morris Gleitzman and
Paul Jennings are available worldwide
from Puffin. See the last page for
details of how to order.

ThE AuTHoRS

Morris Gleitzman and Paul Jennings are Australia's most popular writers for children. They are also very good friends.

**MorRiS
GleiTZmaN**

Phew. We made it. It's been a long and dangerous adventure, with terror and excitement at every turn. And that was just the writing process.

It's been a long journey for you too. Thanks for coming on it with us.

And now we're at the end I can reveal the answer to a mystery I know has been puzzling many of you: how to pronounce Gleitzman. The first part rhymes with bite, fright and goodnight.

PaUL JeNniNGs

So we have finished.

Altogether the six *Wicked!* books contain over seventy-thousand words. That's a lot of writing. And a lot of reading. It's been great fun, but now we've reached the end.

Will you see any more of Dawn and Rory? Morris and I have been talking about a film or TV version.

So you never know.

READ MORE IN PUFFIN

For children of all ages, Puffin represents quality and variety – the very best in publishing today around the world.

For complete information about books available from Puffin – and Penguin – and how to order them, contact us at the appropriate address below. Please note that for copyright reasons the selection of books varies from country to country.

On the worldwide web: www.puffin.co.uk

In the United Kingdom: Please write to *Dept. EP, Penguin Books Ltd, Bath Road, Harmondsworth, West Drayton, Middlesex UB7 ODA*

In the United States: Please write to *Consumer Sales, Penguin USA, P.O. Box 999, Dept. 17109, Bergenfield, New Jersey 07621-0120.* VISA and MasterCard holders call 1-800-253-6476 to order Penguin titles

In Canada: Please write to *Penguin Books Canada Ltd, 10 Alcorn Avenue, Suite 300, Toronto, Ontario M4V 3B2*

In Australia: Please write to *Penguin Books Australia Ltd, P.O. Box 257, Ringwood, Victoria 3134*

In New Zealand: Please write to *Penguin Books (NZ) Ltd, Private Bag 102902, North Shore Mail Centre, Auckland 10*

In India: Please write to *Penguin Books India Pvt Ltd, 706 Eros Apartments, 56 Nehru Place, New Delhi 110 019*

In the Netherlands: Please write to *Penguin Books Netherlands bv, Postbus 3507, NL-1001 AH Amsterdam*

In Germany: Please write to *Penguin Books Deutschland GmbH, Metzlerstrasse 26, 60594 Frankfurt am Main*

In Spain: Please write to *Penguin Books S. A., Bravo Murillo 19, 1° B, 28015 Madrid*

In Italy: Please write to *Penguin Italia s.r.l., Via Felice Casati 20, I–20124 Milano*

In France: Please write to *Penguin France S. A., 17 rue Lejeune, F–31000 Toulouse*

In Japan: Please write to *Penguin Books Japan, Ishikiribashi Building, 2–5–4, Suido, Bunkyo-ku, Tokyo 112*

In South Africa: Please write to *Longman Penguin Southern Africa (Pty) Ltd, Private Bag X08, Bertsham 2013*